BACK AGAINST THE WALL WORKBOOK

Book Study

Author Tamera Kelly

Cover designed by Cover Designer

This workbook compliments "Back Against the Wall", which is a work of fiction. Names, characters, places, and incidents either are products of the author's imagination or are used fictitiously. Any resemblance to actual persons, living or dead, events, or locales is entirely coincidental.

Author Name
Visit my website at www.atkelly.com

Printed in the United States of America

First Printing: July 2020
Amazon/KDP

ISBN-13 : 978-1-7354394-1-9

CONTENTS

Back Against the Wall Characters 4

Diamond Davenport 5

M'Kenzie Davenport 7

Porsha Porter 9

Precious Porter 11

Jackson Porter 13

Caden Jones 14

Discussion Topics 15

Challenges of Being An Entrepreneur 16

Workplace Relationships 17

Challenges of Mental Illness 18

Challenges of Abuse 19

Marital Infidelity 20

Jealousy and Envy and Its Results 21

Challenges of Being a Sports Spouse and Child 22

Role of Abstinence in Relationships 23

Parental Examples and How they Affect Children 24

Challenges of Being a Teen Parent 25

Right and Wrong Reasons for Being in a Relationship (Married or Not) 26

BACK AGAINST THE WALL CHARACTERS

Character Analysis

DIAMOND DAVENPORT

Profile:
- Single mother of M'Kenzie
- Former NFL wife (divorcee)
- Real estate agency owner
- Upper middle class
- Financially strained, yet not broke
- Workplace relationship with a married man

Discussion Topics
• Workplace relationships
• Being a sports spouse
• Challenges of being a business owner
• Infidelity in marriage

How do I relate to Diamond?

_____

_____

_____

_____

_____

_____

_____

_____

Questions to ask myself:
1. What struggles do you share?
2. What have they done to overcome their situation that you can do to overcome yours?
3. How would you handle the situations that Diamond is in/dealing with?
4. How could Diamond have handled her situation differently?

5. How can what happened with Diamond help you with a relationship problem that you are having?
6. What has been your experience with Diamond's situation?
7. Do you feel like Diamond's relationship with Precious could've been saved? If so, how? If not, why not?

M'KENZIE DAVENPORT

Profile:

- Daughter of Diamond
- Daughter of an NFL player
- Popular
- Private school educated; senior in high school
- Street savvy
- In a relationship with Caden
- Protector of those she loves
- Best friend to Porsha

Discussion Topics
• Role of abstinence in relationships • Parental examples and how they affect children • Being a sports child

How do I relate to M'Kenzie?

_____

_____

_____

_____

_____

_____

_____

_____

_____

Questions to ask myself:

1. What struggles do you share?
2. What have they done to overcome their situation that you can do to overcome yours?
3. How would you handle the situations that M'Kenzie is in/dealing with?
4. How could M'Kenzie have handled her situation differently?

5. How can what happened with M'Kenzie help you with a relationship problem that you are having?
6. What has been your experience with M'Kenzie's situation?
7. Do you feel like M'Kenzie's relationships with Porsha and Caden could've been saved? If so, how? If not, why not?

PORSHA PORTER

Profile:

- Daughter of Precious and Jackson
- Best friend of M'Kenzie
- Teen mom of son, Kyle, at 15
- Public school educated; senior in high school
- Jealous of M'Kenzie
- Broken relationship with her mother
- In love with Caden, yet treasures friendship with M'Kenzie
- People pleaser (keeps secrets to preserve relationships)

Discussion Topics
• Challenges of being a teen parent
• Role of abstinence in relationships
• Parental examples and how they affect children
• Jealousy and envy and its results
• Being a people pleaser (keeping secrets to preserve relationships)

How do I relate to Porsha?

_____
_____
_____
_____
_____
_____
_____
_____

Questions to ask myself:
1. What struggles do you share?
2. What have they done to overcome their situation that you can do to overcome yours?

3. How would you handle the situations that Porsha is in/dealing with?
4. How could Porsha have handled her situation differently?
5. How can what happened with Porsha help you with a relationship problem that you are having?
6. What has been your experience with Porsha's situation?
7. Do you feel like Porsha's relationship with her parents, M'Kenzie, and Caden could've been saved? If so, how? If not, why not?

PRECIOUS PORTER

Profile:

- Wife of Jackson and stay-at-home mother of Porsha and one son
- Best friend to Diamond
- Mentally unstable (schizophrenic)
- Insecure and vengeful
- Tainted past due to abuse
- Flamboyant

Discussion Topics
• Challenges of mental illness (in self and relationships)
• Challenges of abuse (insecurity, trust issues, homicidal and suicidal thoughts)
• Right and wrong reasons for being in a relationship (married or not)
• Marital infidelity

How do I relate to Precious?

_____
_____
_____
_____
_____
_____
_____
_____

Questions to ask myself:
1. What struggles do you share?
2. What have they done to overcome their situation that you can do to overcome yours?
3. How would you handle the situations that Precious is in/dealing with?
4. How could Precious have handled her situation differently?
5. How can what happened with Precious help you with a relationship problem that you are having?
6. What has been your experience with Precious's situation?

7. Do you feel like Precious's relationship with Porsha, Diamond, and Jackson could've been saved? If so, how? If not, why not?

JACKSON PORTER

Profile:

- Husband of Precious and Father to Porsha and one son
- Entrepreneur
- Married for the wrong reason
- Secretly in love with Diamond

Discussion Topics
• Challenges of mental illness (in family relationships)
• Right and wrong reason for being in a relationship (married or not)
• Marital infidelity

How do I relate to Jackson?

_____
_____
_____
_____
_____
_____
_____
_____

Questions to ask myself:
1. What struggles do you share?
2. What have they done to overcome their situation that you can do to overcome yours?
3. How would you handle the situations that Jackson is in/dealing with?
4. How could Jackson have handled her situation differently?
5. How can what happened with Jackson help you with a relationship problem that you are having?
6. What has been your experience with Jackson's situation?
7. Do you feel like Jackson's relationship with Precious and Porsha could've been saved? If so, how? If not, why not?

CADEN JONES

Profile:
- Boyfriend of M'Kenzie
- #1 NFL draft pick
- Accomplished
- Affluent family

Discussion Topics
• Challenges of being a teen parent
• Role of abstinence in relationships
• Being a people pleaser (keeping secrets to preserve relationships)
• Being a professional athlete

How do I relate to Caden?

_____
_____
_____
_____
_____
_____
_____
_____

Questions to ask myself:
1. What struggles do you share?
2. What have they done to overcome their situation that you can do to overcome yours?
3. How would you handle the situations that Caden is in/dealing with?
4. How could Caden have handled her situation differently?
5. How can what happened with Caden help you with a relationship problem that you are having?
6. What has been your experience with Caden's situation?
7. Do you feel like Caden's relationship with the NFL and his coaches, his parents, M'Kenzie and Diamond, Porsha, and Precious could've been saved? If so, how? If not, why not?

DISCUSSION TOPICS

Breaking Down the Book and Characters

CHALLENGES OF BEING AN ENTREPRENEUR

Characters:
1. Diamond
    a. Financially strained, yet not broke—real estate slump
    b. Real estate agency owner
2. Jackson
    a. Networking professional
    b. Construction company owner—does work for diamond

Questions I Need to Ask:
1. What struggles do you share?
2. What have they done to overcome their situation that you can do to overcome yours?
3. How would you handle the situations that they're in/dealing with?
4. What has been your experience with their situation?

WORKPLACE RELATIONSHIPS

Characters:

1. Diamond and Nigel
   a. Nigel is Diamond's attorney for her business
   b. Nigel is married to Chasity, whom Diamond HATES
   c. The relationship isn't full-fledged, yet is physical
   d. Diamond dresses to attract Nigel's attention

Questions I Need to Ask:

1. What struggles do you share?
2. What have they done to overcome that you can do?
3. How would you handle the situations that they're in/dealing with?
4. How could they have handled their situation differently?
5. How can what happened with them help you with a relationship problem you are having?
6. What has been your experience with their situation?
7. Do you feel like Nigel and Chasity's marriage will end due to the relationship? Why or why not?

CHALLENGES OF MENTAL ILLNESS

1. Areas
   a. Within self
   b. Within relationships
2. Characters
   a. Precious
      i. Abused as a child
      ii. Killed her abuser
      iii. Very flamboyant and vengeful as a result
      iv. Insecure in marriage due to abuse and husband's affair
      v. Labeled as schizophrenic due to hearing voices
      vi. Not taking psychotropic meds for the condition
   b. Jackson
      i. Spouse of an abused wife
      ii. Target of insecurity
      iii. Infidelity as a coping mechanism
      iv. Stayed out late due to wife's rants and raves

Questions I Need to Ask:
1. What struggles do you share?
2. What have they done to overcome that you can do?
3. How would you handle the situations that they're in/dealing with?
4. How could they have handled their situation differently?
5. How can what happened with them help you with a relationship problem you are having?
6. What has been your experience with their situation?
7. Do you feel like Jackson would have cheated had Precious developed the right coping mechanisms with help? Why or why not?

CHALLENGES OF ABUSE

1. Areas
   a. Developing insecurity
   b. Trust issues
   c. Homicidal and suicidal thoughts
2. Characters
   a. Precious
      i. Abused as a child
      ii. Killed her abuse
      iii. Insecure in marriage due to abuse and husband's affair
      iv. Plots to poison her husband
   b. Jackson
      i. Spouse of an abused wife
      ii. Target of insecurity

Questions I Need to Ask:

1. What struggles do you share?
2. What have they done to overcome that you can do?
3. How would you handle the situations that they're in/dealing with?
4. How could they have handled their situation differently?
5. How can what happened with them help you with a relationship problem you are having?
6. What has been your experience with their situation?
7. Do you think Precious was really responsible for Jackson's sudden sickness? If so, how? If not, why not?

MARITAL INFIDELITY

1. Area—the potential reason for Diamond's divorce
2. Characters
    a. Precious and Jackson
        i. Jackson was unfaithful
        ii. Precious followed her instincts and followed him
        iii. Precious beats the other woman nearly to death and threatens her

Questions I Need to Ask:

1. What struggles do you share?
2. What have they done to overcome that you can do?
3. How would you handle the situations that they're in/dealing with?
4. How could they have handled their situation differently?
5. How can what happened with them help you with a relationship problem you are having?
6. What has been your experience with their situation?
7. Do you feel like Diamond would've had an affair with Nigel if things worked out?
8. Why do you think Jackson cheated?

JEALOUSY AND ENVY AND ITS RESULTS

Characters:

1. Porsha
   a. Jealous of M'Kenzie
      i. Her life
      ii. Her relationship with her mother
      iii. Her relationship with Caden
   b. Acted out of jealousy by sleeping with Caden
   c. Ruined M'Kenzie and Caden's relationship
2. Precious
   a. Jealous of Diamond's life and business
   b. Insecure due to Jackson's affair
   c. The potential reason for Diamond's disappearance

Questions I Need to Ask:

1. What struggles do you share?
2. What have they done to overcome that you can do?
3. How would you handle the situations that they're in/dealing with?
4. How could they have handled their situation differently?
5. How can what happened with them help you with a relationship problem you are having?
6. What has been your experience with their situation?
9. Do you feel like Nigel and Chasity's marriage will end due to the relationship? Why or why not?

CHALLENGES OF BEING A SPORTS SPOUSE AND CHILD

Characters
1. Diamond
    a. Divorced from NFL player
    b. Moved away to starts a new life for her and M'Kenzie
    c. Struggled with relationships
2. M"Kenzie
    a. Societal expectations
    b. Saw her mother's future as her own
    c. Doesn't want Caden to go to the NFL
3. Caden
    a. #1 NFL draft pick
    b. Wants a normal life with M'Kenzie
    c. Deals with pressure of performing overshadowing everything
    d. News of being Kyle's father shakes him up
    e. Fears being seen as just another athlete with skeletons in the closet

Questions I Need to Ask:
1. What struggles do you share?
2. What have they done to overcome that you can do?
3. How would you handle the situations that they're in/dealing with?
4. How could they have handled their situation differently?
5. How can what happened with them help you with a relationship problem you are having?
6. What has been your experience with their situation?
4. Do you think Caden will be forced to make the tough decision of being with his family or staying with M'Kenzie? Will it impact his NFL career?

ROLE OF ABSTINENCE IN RELATIONSHIPS

Areas:
1. M'Kenzie is a virgin, but Caden is not
2. Caden agrees to abstinence
3. Diamond lovingly admonishes her daughter to wait until marriage
4. M'Kenzie keeps Porsha's life struggles at the forefront of her mind

Questions I Need to Ask:
1. What struggles do you share?
2. What have they done to overcome that you can do?
3. How would you handle the situations that they're in/dealing with?
4. How could they have handled their situation differently?
5. How can what happened with them help you with a relationship problem you are having?
6. What has been your experience with their situation?
7. Do you feel like Porsha's life struggles were really the deterrent to premarital sex or was it M'Kenzie's relationship with her mother?

PARENTAL EXAMPLES AND HOW THEY AFFECT CHILDREN

Areas:
1. M'Kenzie fears having the same relationship result as her mother with Caden going to the NFL
2. Porsha resents her mother and is embarrassed by her flamboyance
3. Porsha is jealous of M'Kenzie's relationship with her mother

Questions I Need to Ask:

1. What struggles do you share?
2. What have they done to overcome that you can do?
3. How would you handle the situations that they're in/dealing with?
4. How could they have handled their situation differently?
5. How can what happened with them help you with a relationship problem you are having?
6. What has been your experience with their situation?
7. Do you feel like Precious and Diamond did what was necessary to show their daughters how NOT to make the same mistakes they did?

CHALLENGES OF BEING A TEEN PARENT

Characters:

1. Porsha
   a. Sleeps with Caden to try and win him over because she liked him first and thought he liked her just as much
   b. Misses cycle for 4 months and doesn't notice
   c. Pregnant at 15 and lies about it, but it's confirmed at the doctor
   d. Deals with parental disappointment
   e. Protects Caden by saying Johnathan is the father, but a DNA test proves otherwise
   f. Sets out to have Caden in her life by any means necessary
   g. Has her little brother and Jackson as father figures her son

2. Caden
   a. Teased Porsha growing up because he was trying to get M'Kenzie's attention
   b. Unaware he is Kyle's father for two years
   c. "I only hit that once", but he knows he's the father
   d. Feels his future with the NFL is in jeopardy
   e. Knows his relationship with M'Kenzie is in jeopardy
   f. Comes clean to M'Kenzie and worries he'll lose her
   g. Comes clean to his parents, who pay Porsha and Precious off to stay quiet

Questions I Need to Ask:

1. What struggles do you share?
2. What have they done to overcome that you can do?
3. How would you handle the situations that they're in/dealing with?
4. How could they have handled their situation differently?
5. How can what happened with them help you with a relationship problem you are having?
6. What has been your experience with their situation?
7. What ultimate sacrifice will have to be made here?

RIGHT AND WRONG REASONS FOR BEING IN A RELATIONSHIP (MARRIED OR NOT)

Characters:
1. Precious
   a. Wanted to keep Jackson because no other man had treated her the way he did
   b. Jackson was careless and got Precious pregnant
   c. Jackson marries Precious because she's pregnant, has an affair, and is secretly in love with Diamond
2. Porsha
   a. Slept with Caden, but kept it quiet to preserve her friendship
   b. Tried to make a family with Johnathan, but it didn't work
   c. Wanted Caden badly enough to jeopardize her friendship with M'Kenzie

Questions I Need to Ask:
1. What struggles do you share?
2. What have they done to overcome that you can do?
3. How would you handle the situations that they're in/dealing with?
4. How could they have handled their situation differently?
5. How can what happened with them help you with a relationship problem you are having?
6. What has been your experience with their situation?
7. What role did pressure play in these situations?